White Lightning

White Lightning

Robin and Chris Lawrie

Illustrated by
Robin Lawrie

Acknowledgements

The authors and publishers would like to thank Julia Francis, Hereford Diocesan Deaf Church lay co-chaplain, for her help with the sign language in the *Chain Gang* books.

Published by Evans Brothers Limited
2A Portman Mansions
Chiltern Street
London W1U 6NR

Printed in Hong Kong

British Library Cataloguing in Publication data.

Lawrie, Robin
  White Lightning. – (The Chain Gang)
  1. Slam Duncan (Fictitious character) – Juvenile fiction
  2. All terrain cycling – Juvenile fiction 3. Adventure stories
  4. Children's stories
  I. Title II. Lawrie, Chris
  823.9'14[J]

ISBN 0 237 52109 1

Hi, my name is "Slam" Duncan. I belong to a downhill mountain bike racing team called "The Chain Gang".

There's Aziz, or "Dozy", who is my best mate. Then there's Larry, who broke his leg early in the season, Andy, who's deaf and uses sign language. And then there's Fionn.

She's a brilliant downhiller but she can be a bit weird. She actually likes horses! She rides this big, white, monster called Baggage.

5

Most downhill courses end with
some big jumps
in the run-out field
near the finish.
They provide
lots of thrills
for the crowd.

Oooooooohhh!!

6

Usually, they are just big piles of dirt on the side of a hill.

But they need practising.
That's why me and the gang
build practice jumps on
Larry's uncle's hill farm.

Single

Double

Table top

This can cause problems with the local horse riders. They reckon our jumps are on their bridle paths.*

C'mon, lads, how're we supposed to take horses over that lot?

Uh oh!

They'll have to go!

Next day . . .

Oh no! Somebody's smashed our jumps!

This'll be Fionn and her horsey mates.

That's it! She's out of the gang.

*A bridle path is a track for horses.

**Why? Why?

9

8:00 a.m. The next Saturday – the day of the last race in the Westland Super Series. Time for some practice. Luckily, we had some race transport because it was a very long walk to the top.

* What's the time? ** Eight o'clock.

Fionn always needed help to lift her bike on to the trailer because she is so small. But today, nobody was talking to her.

Finally, she said:

That did it.

Fionn had had enough.

She turned round and rode home.

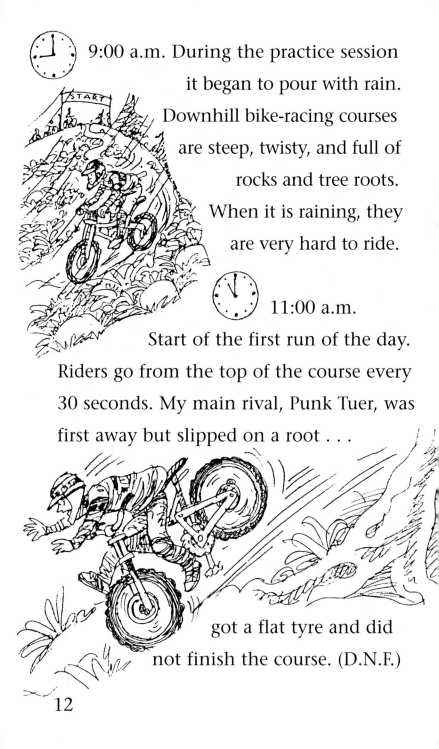

9:00 a.m. During the practice session it began to pour with rain. Downhill bike-racing courses are steep, twisty, and full of rocks and tree roots. When it is raining, they are very hard to ride.

11:00 a.m.

Start of the first run of the day. Riders go from the top of the course every 30 seconds. My main rival, Punk Tuer, was first away but slipped on a root . . .

got a flat tyre and did not finish the course. (D.N.F.)

12

On my run, I rode my
socks off . . .

but
could only
manage the sixth
fastest time of the morning.
Andy got the third fastest,
Dozy got the second fastest, but
Punk's "Tuer Racing" team mate,
Dyno Sawyer, got the fastest time.

12:45 p.m. The Tuer Racing team
mechanic changed
Punk's tyre . . .

. . . while he and Dyno changed into some
nice, dry, racing kit in the team van.
Then they cycled over the bridge
into Shabberley
for some crisps
and pop.

It was still raining.

Meanwhile, I decided to have one more practice run. But, as I was unloading my bike from the transport trailer at the top of the course . . .

I dropped it, and bent the front wheel. I knew I had a spare one at home, but I would have to be quick. The second timed run started at 2:00 p.m.

RATS!

1:00 p.m. I started running down the fire road towards Shabberley. I had to be back at the top by 1:50 p.m. with my new wheel, or else I'd miss my second run. It was going to be close.

As I was steaming through the race village on the way to the bridge, I noticed Fionn, and Baggage, outside the administration tent. She seemed to be writing down our times.

It was still raining.

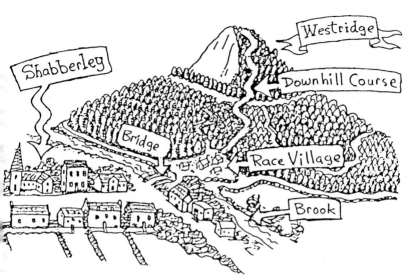

When I got to the bridge, the water was roaring under it. In fact, it was starting to roar over it, as well.

I should have guessed what would happen.

1:45 p.m. Punk, Dyno and I got back to the bridge just in time to see it get washed away.

Second run in 15 minutes.

Now what?

Punk and Dyno decided the only
way to get back across the brook
was to jump it.
They climbed up
the bank . . .

. . . shot back down at high speed
and, using what was left
of the bridge
as a ramp . . .

. . . made a beautiful take-off,

got big air . . .

but not enough.

Punk and Dyno could swim
but their bikes couldn't.
They climbed out
of the water,
but their bikes
were never
seen again.

21

I was still wondering what to do when . . .

like a bolt

of white lightning,

Fionn and Baggage jumped the brook.

After the way we had treated her I was

amazed she still cared.

I was never very good at maths,
but Fionn showed me
her sums.

Now do you get it?

Wow!

Race	1	2	3	4	5	Total (4 Best)
Punk	100					
Dyno	99	-	89			
Larry	93	100	88	100	99	388
Slam	92	99	-	99	98	384
Aziz	94	98	87	96	100	98	387
Andy	91	-	98	97	97	389
		98	98	96	383	

Next thing I knew,
I was jumping up
behind Fionn
and we were off!

*1st = 100 pts.
2nd = 99 pts.
3rd = 98 pts, and so on.

I've done some big jumps in my time,
but this was mad.
We soared over Shabberley Brook.
I could see the water foaming below.
We seemed to be
in the air for minutes.
I knew then that I would
never look down
on horse riders –
or girls – again . . .
even small
ones!

We landed light as a feather
and were off up the fire road
in a flash.

1.55 p.m. Five minutes until the start of the second round of runs. My mates on the transport trailer couldn't believe their eyes. We were going to make it!

We got to the start line
with two minutes
to spare.

I had the new wheel on
in 20 seconds flat.

Fionn's support and my amazing ride
on Baggage had really fired me up.
I was the last rider away . . .
got a good start . . .
and rode
like a demon.

GO, SLAM!

Through the
rocky section . . .

over the
dropoffs . . .

through
the slippery,
slithery, slidy,
root section, with the cheers
of the crowd ringing in my ears.
I knew I was
going well,
but not
how well
until . . .

I crossed the finish line – looked at
the timing board and saw . . .

Even before the official series results
were pinned up, Fionn had done the sums.

Race	1	2	3	4	5	6	TOTAL (4 BEST)	
Punk	100	—	89	100	99	—	388	
Dyno	99	—	88	99	98	91	387	
Larry	93	100	—	—	—	—	193	
Slam	92	99	87	96	100	100	395	1st
Aziz	94	98	97	97	97	99	391	2nd
Andy	91	—	98	98	96	98	390	3rd

I had scored a first for the race and
a first for the series. Dozy was second
in both, and Andy, third.

Even though 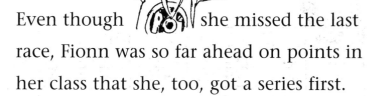 she missed the last
race, Fionn was so far ahead on points in
her class that she, too, got a series first.

Larry still had a broken leg
but said: Watch out next year!

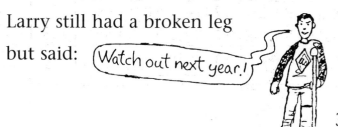

31

Next day, Dozy asked me to go with him
to see Fionn. He didn't dare go on his own.

Fionn had no idea what it might be

but she soon found out.

Just what she had
always wanted.